Published in Great Britain in MMXXI by
Scribblers, an imprint of
The Salariya Book Company Ltd
25 Marlborough Place, Brighton BN1 1UB
www.salariya.com

ISBN: 978-1-913337-96-4

© The Salariya Book Company Ltd MMXXI

All rights reserved. No part of this publication may be reproduced, stored in or introduced into a retrieval system or transmitted in any form, or by any means (electronic, mechanical, photocopying, recording or otherwise) without the written permission of the publisher. Any person who does any unauthorised act in relation to this publication may be liable to criminal prosecution and civil claims for damages.

1 3 5 7 9 8 6 4 2

A CIP catalogue record for this book is available from the British Library.

This book is sold subject to the conditions that it shall not, by way of trade or otherwise, be lent, resold, hired out, or otherwise circulated without the publisher's prior consent in any form of binding or cover other than that in which it is published and without similar condition being imposed on the subsequent purchaser.

Editor: **Nick Pierce**

Visit
www.salariya.com
for our online catalogue and
free fun stuff.

PAPER FROM SUSTAINABLE FORESTS

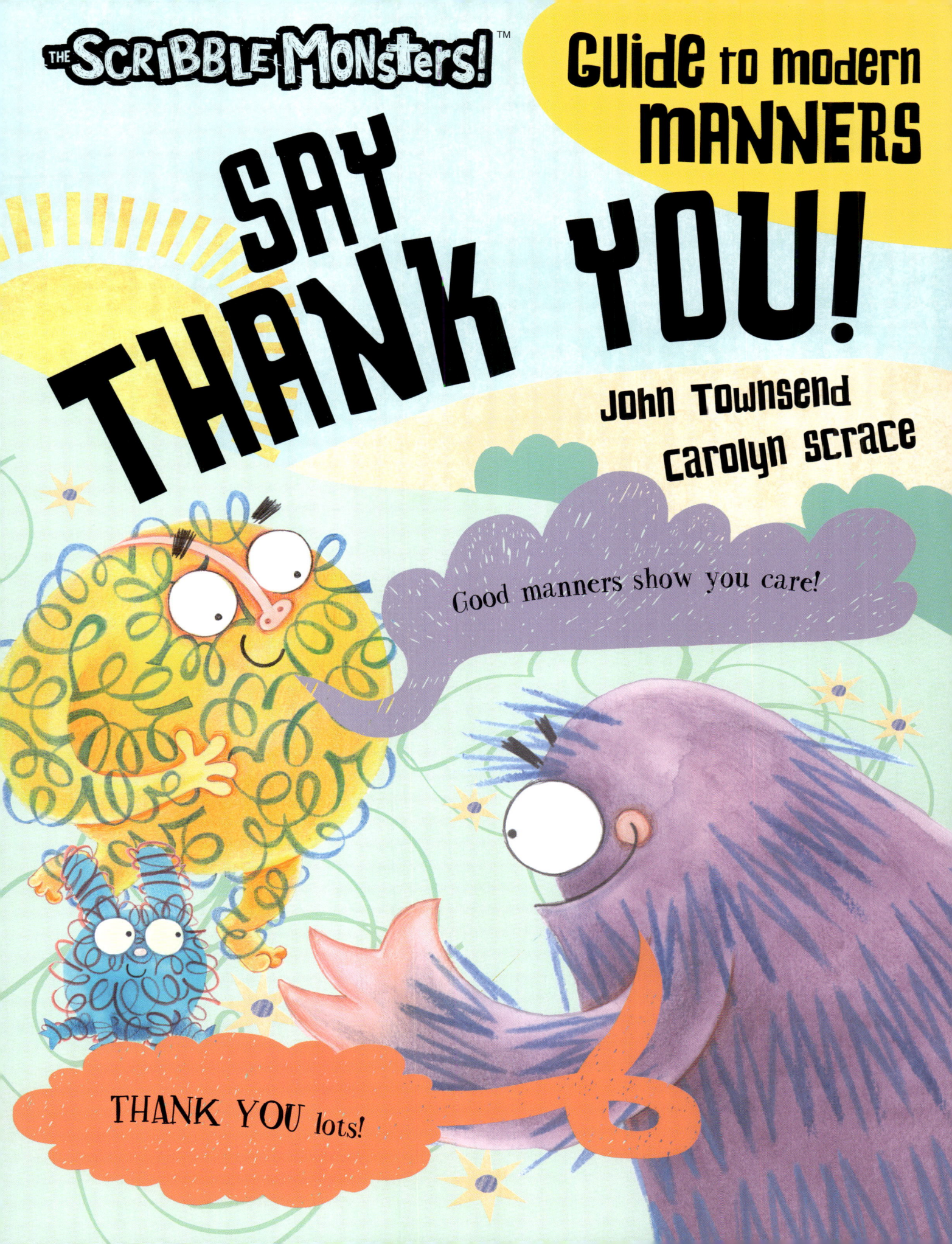

We're the friendly Scribble Monsters,
We scribble lots of lines
And write how manners can be fun
On all our scribbly signs.

Thanks a bundle!
Thanks a bunch!

Thank you lots!

What everyone knows is:
You don't need red roses,
But just a big smile
For a **thank you** with style!

Some little children can forget
To leave kind words behind them...
We're here to scribble our advice
And find ways to remind them.

Smudge will always say a **'thank you'**
Each time we throw a ball.
And Spotty gives a grateful lick,
A wagging tail and all!

The Scribble Monsters give awards
To children who delight,
By saying 'Thank You' all the time
And being so polite.

Thank You!

THANK YOU!

THANK YOU!

Make someone's day - say 'Thank You'.

Would you like to come and party?

Nibs is quite a dancer.
It looks like Blot is lost for words...

'Thank You' is the answer!

It's easy to forget to say
Those two important words.
'**Thank You**' is even what is sung
By all those chirpy birds!

Poor Inky stumbles and falls flat,
It feels like a disaster...

Till Pablo bathes the painful knee
And puts on a clean plaster.

Inky wants to send a 'Thank You'
In a **thank you** letter.

Nibs has given me a letter –
Look at what I've got.
I really don't know what to say.

Dear Blot
I would like you to have my skates
love Nibs

Thank You would say a lot.

H.B. cleans up Nibs' smudges,
Each splodge and messy blot.

I really don't know what to say.

Dear Blot,
would
you to eat
love
Nibs

Thank You would say a lot.

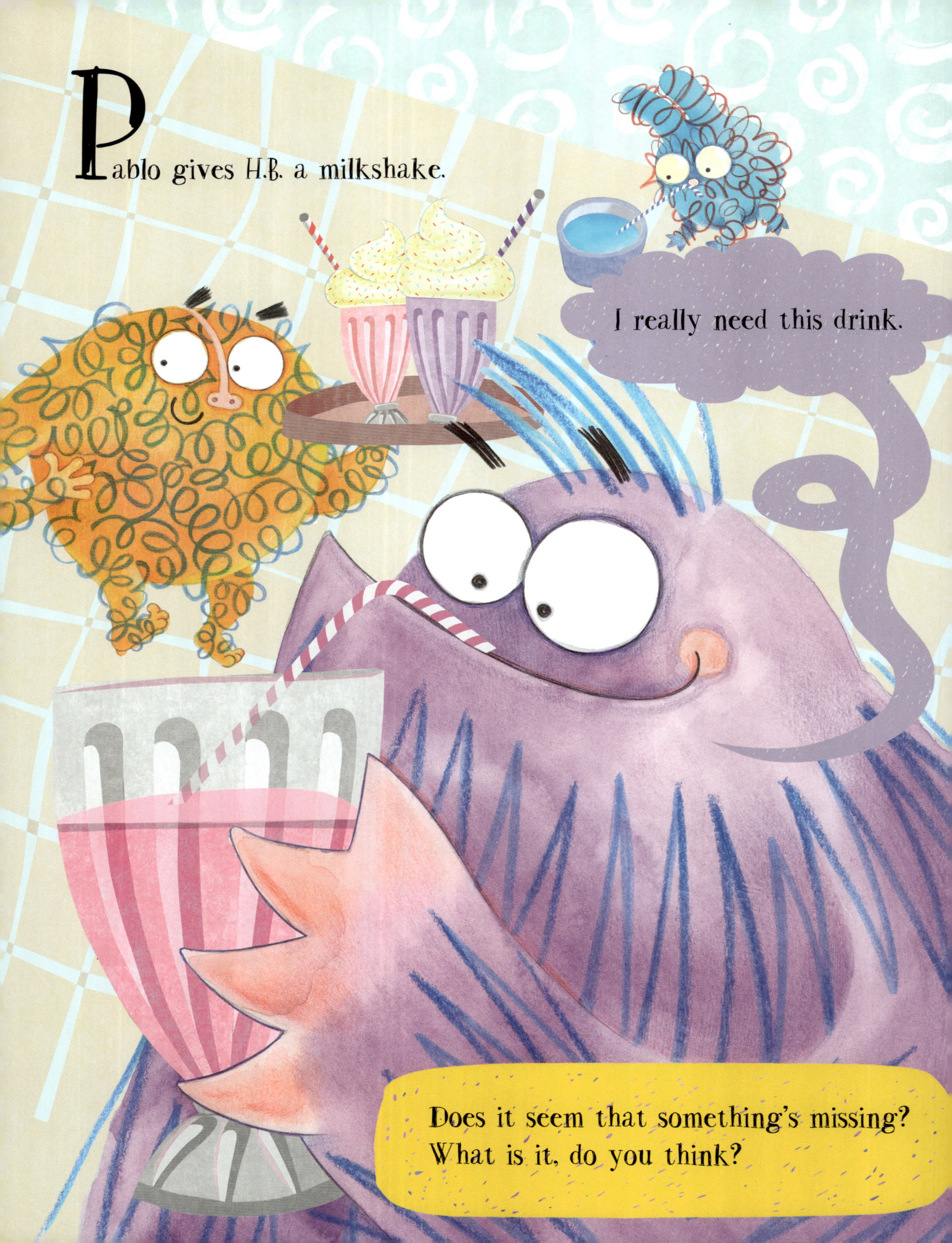

Pablo gives H.B. a milkshake.

I really need this drink.

Does it seem that something's missing? What is it, do you think?

Inky has a lot of presents,
And makes a special list
Of everyone to send a card to...

Great, I love presents

Blot
18 Scribble Street
Monsterville

MY LIST
Blot
H.B.
Pablo
Nibs
Smudge

What words has Inky missed?

Thank you, all you Scribble Monsters
For every short reminder
To help us say our 'Thank Yous' and
Be a little kinder.

Thank You for the time you give me.

Those words are good to hear.

Thank You for the words of kindness
You whisper in my ear.

Bedtime is when Smudge gives cuddles,
A pet's own special way
To say

Thank You for your love
And all you've shared today.

HAVE YOU HEARD THE MAGIC WORD?

THANK YOU so much!

GOOD MANNERS ARE FREE!

THANK YOU!

The Scribble Monsters wave goodbye
With friendly flags and banners
To help all children to remember
Those SCRIBBLE MONSTER MANNERS!

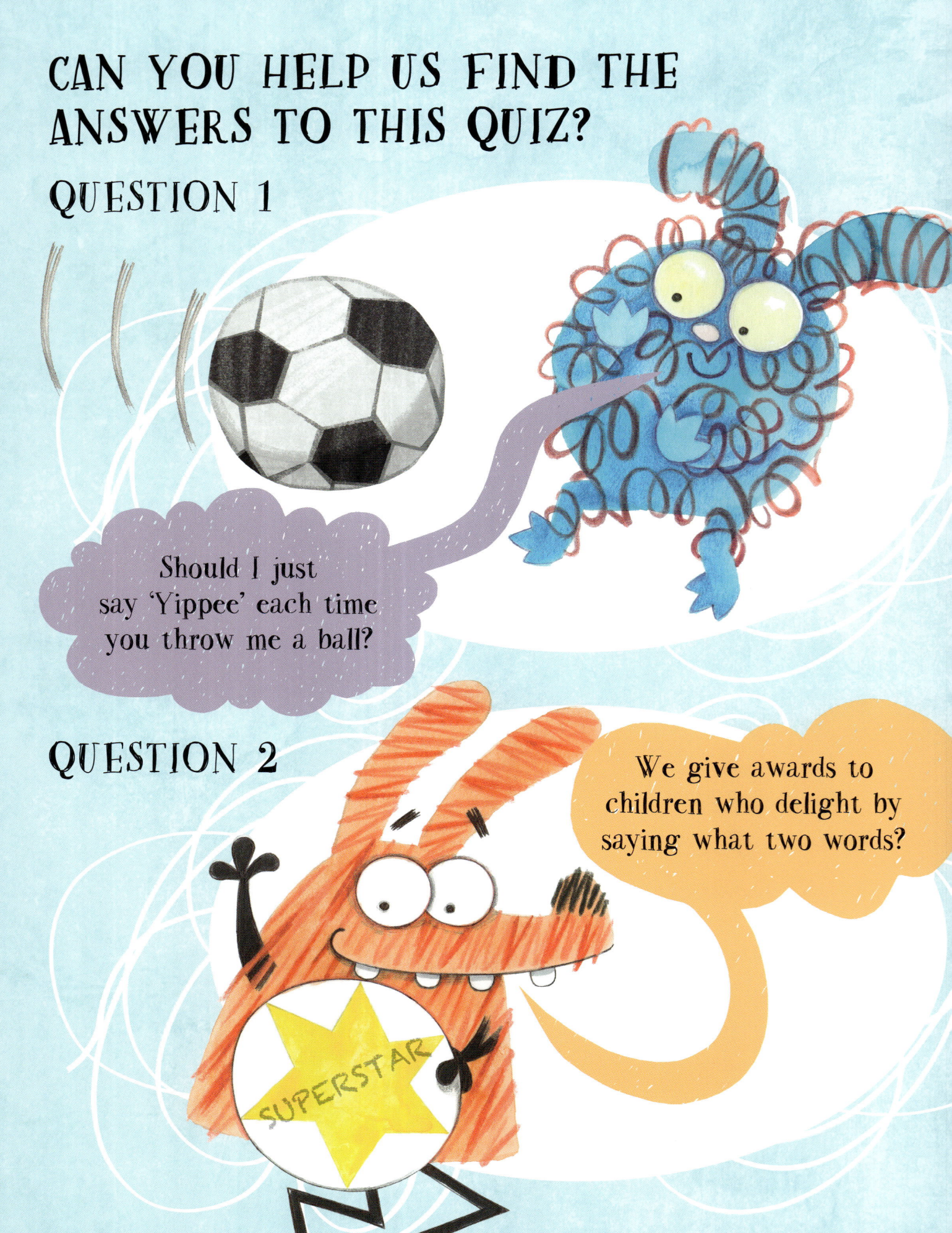

QUESTION 3

I've asked if Blot would like to come to a party. Should Blot answer 'Oh yes'?

QUESTION 4

What sort of letter should I write to Pablo, for helping me and making me feel better?

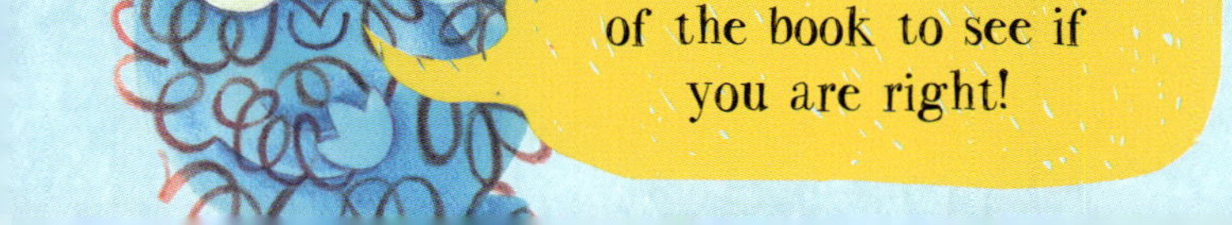

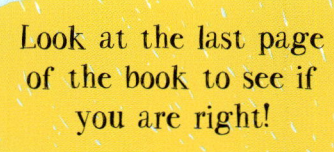

Look at the last page of the book to see if you are right!

MORE MONSTER QUESTIONS

QUESTION 5

When I gave H.B. a milkshake, he said 'I really need this drink'. What words are missing, do you think?

QUESTION 6

I am sending a card to everyone who has given me a present. Do you think what I have written in this card is alright?

QUESTION 7

At bedtime, did I just fall asleep without thanking my friend?

QUESTION 8

What makes us thrilled, with dancing in the ranks?

Look at the last page of the book to see if you are right!

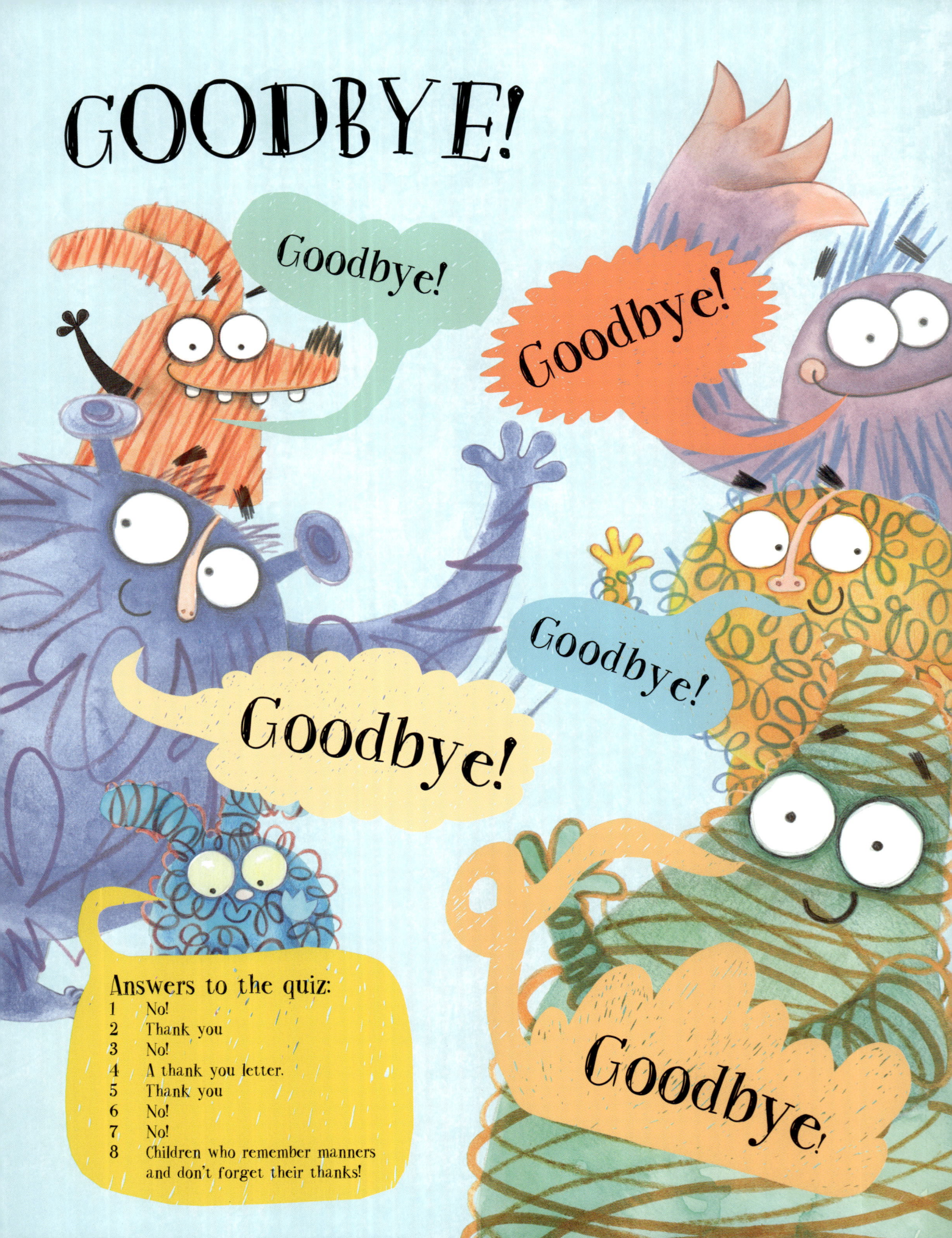